Backcourt Battle

An Up2U Character Education Adventure

by Rich Wallace

illustrated by Chris King

WITHDRAWN

Calico

An Imprint of Magic Wagon
abdopublishing.com

For Hector and Jameyre. -RW

abdopublishing.com

Printed in the United States of America, North Mankato, Minnesota.
052017
092017

 THIS BOOK CONTAINS
RECYCLED MATERIALS

Written by Rich Wallace
Illustrated by Chris King
Edited by Bridget O'Brien
Design Contributors: Christina Doffing and Laura Mitchell

Publisher's Cataloging-in-Publication Data

Names: Wallace, Rich, author. | King, Chris, illustrator.
Title: Backcourt battle: an Up2U character education adventure / by Rich
    Wallace ; illustrated by Chris King.
Other titles: An Up2U character education adventure
Description: Minneapolis, MN : Magic Wagon, 2018. | Series: Up2U
    adventures
Summary: After the starting point guard sprains his ankle, Jamere steps in
    until his rival teammate returns for the championship, but with both
    boys expecting to be starters, Coach asks Jamere to decide who will
    play and it's up to the reader to choose the solution.
Identifiers: LCCN 2017930881 | ISBN 9781532130281 (lib. bdg.) |
    ISBN 9781614798651 (ebook) | ISBN 9781614798705 (Read-to-me
    ebook)
Subjects: LCSH: Plot-your-own stories. | Basketball--Juvenile fiction.
Classification: DDC [Fic]--dc23
LC record available at http://lccn.loc.gov/2017930881

TABLE OF CONTENTS

CHAPTER

→ 1 ←

Ignore the Noise

Jamere leaned forward. He hadn't played at all, but his hands were sweating. His team clung to a narrow lead.

The fans cheered as Jamere's teammate Kyle tossed in a three-point shot. Fairfield led by five with two minutes left.

Hector nudged Jamere. "We're going to win!"

Jamere forced a smile. Kyle was playing a great game, but it was hard for Jamere to be happy. *I should be out there*, he thought.

Jamere and Kyle had been rivals for a long time. They'd pitched against each other in Little

League. They'd also battled in YMCA soccer games. When Coach Sanchez named Kyle the starting point guard, Jamere almost dropped off the team. But Jamere wasn't a quitter. He kept working hard in practice.

Kyle nailed another three-pointer.

"Wow!" yelled Hector, leaping to his feet. The upset looked certain.

Jamere stood, too. The Westwood point guard raced up the court. Kyle stayed close.

As the guard dribbled into the lane, the Westwood center stepped up and set a hard screen. Kyle smashed into him. The shot went in as Kyle fell to the floor. He grabbed his ankle, letting out a yelp.

Kyle lay on the floor until Coach Sanchez helped him to his feet. He hobbled to the bench and sneered.

"Jamere," Coach said.

Jamere gave Coach a puzzled look.

"Get in there," Coach growled.

Jamere reported to the scorer's table. "I'm in for Kyle," he said.

Jamere nodded to the Westwood point guard, Trey Freeman. He was the best player in the league. Freeman stared him down. The scoreboard read FAIRFIELD 53. VISITORS 45. 1:27. 4Q.

You wanted this chance, Jamere thought. Tight game. An undefeated opponent. Talk about pressure!

Jamere scrambled to get open, but Freeman stayed on him. Derek bounced the ball Jamere's way. Jamere turned and dribbled with Freeman in his face.

Jamere reached the sideline. Freeman had him trapped. He stopped dribbling. *Don't do that*, he scolded himself.

Derek waved his arms. Jamere threw the ball, but Freeman tipped it back. They ran to the ball. Freeman got there first, taking it in stride and swooping toward the basket.

Freeman leaped for a lay-up. Jamere hacked his shoulder. The whistle blew as the ball fell through the net.

"Number two," said the ref, indicating a foul on Jamere.

Freeman made the foul shot. 53–48.

Coach called a time-out. "Settle down, Jamere," he said.

Jamere saw Kyle staring at him. "Don't waste that lead," Kyle said sternly.

"Shut it, Kyle," Coach said. "Relax, Jamere. And Derek, give him some help bringing up the ball."

"Because Freeman will eat him alive," Kyle said.

Coach glared at Kyle.

"I shut Freeman down all day," Kyle said. "Now Jamere goes in there and chokes."

Hector gave Jamere a light punch on the shoulder. "Ignore the noise," he said.

Jamere made the inbounds pass this time, bouncing the ball to Derek. Freeman stayed close as Jamere ran up the court. *Get away from this guy*, Jamere thought. *Shake him.*

Jamere cut to the corner. Then he ran along the baseline under the basket. Freeman mirrored every step.

Derek was in trouble, with two Westwood players hounding him. Jamere looped around behind Derek and yelled for the ball.

Derek ducked low and bounced the ball. Jamere grabbed it.

The whistle blew again.

"Back court," said the ref, reaching for the basketball. Jamere had stepped over the midcourt line.

"Wake up!" Kyle yelled from the bench.

Jamere gulped and looked at the clock. 0:46.

Where was Freeman? Jamere darted toward him. *No open shots*, he thought.

Freeman was quick, and he knew how to get clear. Jamere shadowed him. Freeman dodged left and stepped to the right. He took a quick pass before Jamere could recover.

The three-point shot rippled through the net. Fairfield's lead was only two points.

And now Jamere had to bring the ball up again.

Derek passed. Jamere pivoted. Freeman poked the ball away.

Jamere recovered the ball and elbowed Freeman. *Step up and do something good,* he told himself. He dribbled hard. Passed to Derek. Slipped away from Freeman and took a return pass.

Jamere passed to one of the forwards. The shot glanced off the rim. Westwood grabbed the rebound and called a time-out.

"Tight defense," Coach said as the team gathered around him. "They'll be looking for

Freeman." He pointed to Jamere. "Don't. Leave. Him. Alone."

Sixteen seconds. A basket would force overtime. A three-pointer meant a loss.

Jamere chased Freeman. The same play unfolded that knocked Kyle to the floor. *Bam*!

Jamere stumbled backward as he ran into the Westwood center. He watched in horror as Freeman unleashed a jumper from behind the arc.

The ball bounced off the rim and fell to the side. Jamere let out a sigh of relief.

The horn blew. Game over.

Why didn't it feel like a win?

CHAPTER

2

Bye-Bye?

Jamere walked slowly toward the locker room. His teammates celebrated around him.

"That was tough," Hector said. He fell into step next to Jamere. "Coming in ice-cold off the bench in a tight game."

Jamere shook his head. "Freeman made me look bad."

Hector shrugged. "We won. You made a difference."

"Not much," Jamere replied. He sat on the bench in front of his locker. He took off his jersey. "Barely even sweaty," he said, folding the shirt.

Coach Sanchez gave his usual postgame speech. "We hung on. We beat a good team. But we have a lot of work to do."

"Always work to do," Hector whispered.

Jamere looked around. "Where's Kyle?"

"His parents took him to get an X-ray," Derek said. "That ankle was really swollen."

He might be out of action, Jamere thought. *Does that make me the point guard?*

Coach answered that question before Jamere could ask it. "Expect to start in Thursday's game," he told Jamere. "You did all right tonight. But you need to think more. Be aware."

Hector joked around on the walk home. Jamere stayed quiet.

"We're tied for first. Today's win did it," Hector said, trying to cheer up his friend. "Maybe I'll play if Kyle is out," Hector continued. "You've been saying all season that you should be starting. Now you can prove it."

Jamere agreed, but he didn't feel confident. He hated to admit it. Kyle had done a great job guarding Freeman. Jamere hadn't.

"See you," Jamere said as they reached his street.

Hector ran off. "I need to burn some energy," he called. "Sitting on the bench doesn't exactly tire me out!"

"Come over later!" Jamere called back.

"Can't. Social studies test tomorrow!"

Jamere wasn't worried about the test. He'd review the material after dinner. He was starving.

Jamere's older brother, Micah, was in the kitchen, looking into the refrigerator. "What's up, little brother?" Micah asked.

"We won," Jamere replied. "Where's Mom?"

"She's working late." Micah took out a carton of eggs. "I'm making dinner."

"Eggs again? I had one for breakfast."

"They're easy. Do you have a better idea?"

Jamere swung open the refrigerator door. "There's a carton of leftover rice back here," he said. "We could fry it with something."

"Like eggs," Micah said.

"I guess." Jamere slid open the produce drawer. "Here's some mushrooms."

Micah poured some olive oil into a pan. "We'll make fried-egg sandwiches. My specialty."

"I need them. Tough game today."

"Did you play?" Micah asked.

Jamere nodded. "Important minutes, too." *Well, one important minute,* he thought. "Kyle got hurt."

Micah pointed to the mushrooms. "You want to chop them, or should I?"

"Let me get rid of my stuff," Jamere said. He carried his backpack toward the room he shared with Micah. The apartment was small but cozy, with two bedrooms. Jamere, his mother, and his brother had lived there for three years.

Jamere sat on the bottom bunk and pulled off his sneakers. Trophies lined the two desks. Micah's were mostly for high school basketball and track. Jamere had soccer, basketball, and baseball trophies from the town youth leagues.

This season was different. Jamere was representing the middle school. And he was playing against teams from other towns for the first time.

Micah skipped basketball this year. He'd decided to put all of his efforts into track. With his height and his springy legs, he was one of the best hurdlers in the county.

A note on Jamere's desk caught his eye.

Hi Sweetie. Can't wait to hear about the game. Micah will make dinner. You clean up!

Love, Mom

The game. Make it sound good, he told himself. *So what if Freeman scored six points in about six seconds!*

Jamere picked up one of Micah's basketball trophies.

FAIRFIELD MIDDLE SCHOOL
LEAGUE CHAMPIONS

Jamere wanted one just like that. He wanted to earn it for playing, not by sitting on the bench.

"Come here, Jamere!" Micah called.

Jamere smiled. Micah had been calling him that all his life: "Come here, Jamere." They both loved it.

"How bad is Kyle hurt?" Micah asked.

"He turned his ankle, so I'm starting on Thursday. That's all I know."

"Ankles take a while," Micah said. "At least a week to recover from a sprain. If it's broken, then bye-bye season. I've been through that, remember?"

"Ouch," Jamere said. Micah's basketball season was cut short the year before by a sprain.

Jamere took a bite of his sandwich. He shut his eyes and enjoyed the taste.

"That's why I'm not playing this year," Micah said. "Didn't want to risk another setback. Once you twist an ankle, it's easy to do it again."

Jamere set down his sandwich. He didn't like Kyle much. But he didn't want an injury to keep him off the court. *I just want to beat him fair and square. But I'll take any advantage I can get.*

CHAPTER
→ 3 ←

On Fire

At lunch the next day, Jamere noticed Kyle was on crutches. His ankle was wrapped in a brown bandage.

"Sprained," Hector said. "It'll be a week before he can run."

"How do you know?" Jamere asked.

"I know things." Hector balled up his sandwich wrapper. He shot it toward a trash basket. It fell short.

Jamere crunched up his own wrapper. Then he shot the paper in a high arc. It fell neatly into the basket.

"That's how it's done," Jamere said. "Did you talk to Kyle or what?"

Hector shook his head. "Coach told me. He said I should be ready to work in practice. Looks like I'll move into your backup role."

"Maybe we'll go head-to-head when we scrimmage." Jamere liked that idea. Usually he covered Kyle in practice. That was no fun at all. Too many elbows and too much trash talk.

Jamere kept looking at Kyle. He sat with some of their teammates at a table. Kyle was laughing. He didn't seem upset about his ankle.

Laugh now, Kyle, Jamere thought. *You won't have the starting job when you come back. It's mine.*

At practice, Coach Sanchez told the starters to take the court. "New lineup, obviously," he said. "Jamere's playing the point. Full speed. Smart passes. Same as if Kyle was out there."

Coach sent five others onto the court, including Hector.

"Amateur hour!" Kyle called from the bleachers. "Better go easy on Jamere. He's the weak link."

Coach glared at Kyle. "Try to be supportive, Kyle," he said. "That's what being a team is about."

"Just don't mess up too bad, Jamere," Kyle said. He held up three fingers. "Keep my job warm for three games. Then I'll be back."

Jamere looked away. *He's all talk*, he thought. *Show him.*

Hector took a defensive stance. His hands were up and his eyes on Jamere's waist. They played one-on-one constantly in driveways and at playgrounds. They knew each other's strengths and weaknesses.

Jamere dribbled through his legs and cut right. Hector wasn't fooled. He knocked the ball loose. Jamere recovered it.

"Protect that ball," Coach said.

Jamere passed it to a teammate.

Then Hector stole the ball and brought it up the court. Jamere guarded him closely. But Hector made a nice pass. He burst into the lane for a give-and-go. He easily banked the ball off the backboard for a lay-up.

"Nice play," Jamere mumbled. *Bad start. Settle down.* He knew Hector would get his points. There wasn't much difference between them.

Jamere passed the ball, then cut to the corner. Hector followed the ball. When the center fired it back to Jamere, he was wide open. He drained the three-pointer.

That was the play he needed. He immediately felt better. *Get in a rhythm*, he told himself.

Jamere soon forgot about the burden of being a starter. He made good passes. Played tight defense. And he hit his next three shots, too.

"You're on fire." Hector shook his head. Then he raced up the court with the ball. He ran a give-and-go again, popping in another lay-up.

Back and forth. The starters dominated the action. Hector played well and kept Jamere on his toes. But Jamere kept shooting the lights out. He made seven of his nine shots.

Coach blew his whistle and clapped. "Ten free throws apiece. Good practice."

Jamere took a long drink of water. He wiped his hands on his shirt and caught his breath. He headed for the foul line.

Coach stood behind him while he shot. Jamere hit the first three. Then he missed two in a row. *Concentrate*, he thought. He made his next five.

"Great work, Jamere," Coach said. "We won't miss a beat if you play like that tomorrow."

"I will," Jamere said. He strutted off the court.

In the locker room, Jamere rubbed his hair with a towel. This time his shirt was very sweaty.

"Big game tomorrow," Hector said. "And don't worry. If you get tired, I'll take your place."

Jamere grinned. "I can run all day. You know that. But yeah, you should get some minutes, too. You showed a lot today."

Other players shuffled into the locker room, yanking open their lockers. Jamere pulled on a dry T-shirt. He tried to ignore Kyle, who was heading toward him, supporting himself with his crutches.

"Nice job out there," Kyle said.

Jamere raised his eyebrows. "You serious?"

Kyle let out a *pfft* sound with his lips. "Seriously joking," he said. "You were playing against the third string."

"He still did good," Hector said. "Those shots didn't go in by themselves."

Jamere pointed to Hector. "That's a pretty good third-stringer," he said to Kyle.

Kyle hobbled away. "Enjoy it while you can, Jamere."

"I will. Why don't you stop being such an annoying jerk?"

Kyle laughed. "I'll be back," he said, "stronger than ever."

Jamere turned to Hector. "Maybe," he whispered. "But he has to get past me first. I'll be playing so well that Coach will have no choice but to keep Kyle on the bench."

CHAPTER

→» 4 «←

A Rough Start

On Thursday afternoon, Jamere could hardly sit still on the bus ride to Emerson.

"We'll run them off the court," he said to Hector.

"Play smart," Hector said. "You know what Coach says. Good passes lead to good shots."

Jamere was out of control early in the game. He drove straight for the basket as soon as he got the ball. He didn't even look to pass. The Emerson center blocked his shot.

On the next possession, Jamere tried to make up for it. He dribbled to the corner and sent up a shot. It banged off the rim. Emerson grabbed the rebound and raced up the court for a fast-break lay-up.

Jamere frowned at the scoreboard. He passed the ball to Derek, but immediately called for it back. *Time for a three,* he told himself. He launched a long shot, which barely grazed the rim. The ball rolled out-of-bounds.

"Jamere!"

He turned to see Hector running onto the court. Hector pointed to him. "You're out."

"Really?" The game had barely started.

Coach nodded to the spot next to him on the bench. Jamere sat down hard.

"Ever heard of passing the ball?" Kyle asked. He was sitting a few seats over.

Jamere stared straight ahead. "I was just trying to get us going," he said. "Put up some points."

"You're the weak link in the chain," Kyle said.

Ignore him, Jamere thought.

Coach leaned toward Jamere. "Count our guys on the floor," he said. "Five of them, right? We're not a one-man team."

Jamere blushed. "I know," he mumbled. "Sorry."

"Okay. Let's see how Hector does. Stay ready."

Jamere leaned back. What if Hector played great? Would Jamere's chance be over? *Can't believe I hogged the ball like that*, he thought. *That's not me.*

Fairfield trailed, 15–7, at the end of the first quarter. Jamere hadn't budged from the bench.

"Starting five again," Coach said.

Jamere bumped his fist against Hector's. "Good job," he said.

Hector tapped his own forehead. "Think," he said. "Don't just react."

Jamere didn't try to shoot in the second quarter. He concentrated on playing defense. He passed the ball to his teammates. He made a couple of steals, and Fairfield trimmed the lead. By halftime, they were down by a single point.

"Much better," Coach said. "The point guard runs the show. Take the shots if you're open. But you don't need to force them."

Kyle didn't say anything to Jamere in the locker room. Jamere knew he was the main reason they were back in the game.

Jamere kept passing the ball, working it outside to Derek or inside to Lonnie, the center. Fairfield built a lead. Two points. Four.

Jamere took a pass at the top of the key. He didn't have to think this time. He smoothly shot the ball, and it rippled through the net.

"Three-pointer!" shouted Hector. "We're rolling!"

Emerson called a time-out. Jamere ran to the huddle.

"Keep up that pressure," Coach said. "Let's put this game out of reach."

Jamere scored two more baskets before Hector replaced him late in the fourth quarter. He'd led Fairfield to a 15-point lead with his pinpoint passing.

His teammates cheered as Jamere walked off the court. Except for Kyle, who stayed quiet.

Lonnie and Derek came out of the game at the next whistle, sitting on either side of Jamere.

"Great comeback," Lonnie said.

"You just needed to get into the flow," Derek said. He patted Jamere on the back. "You shook off those nerves."

Jamere was much more relaxed on the bus ride home. He looked back to see where Kyle was sitting. Kyle was four rows behind by himself. He was looking out the window. Everybody else was celebrating the win.

"I think we're better with you at the point," Hector whispered. "Kyle's good, but you keep everybody involved." He laughed. "At least, you did for most of the game. I don't know what that first minute was about."

"Tension," Jamere said. "I wanted to start with a blast. Turned out to be a dud."

"Gave me a chance to show my stuff," Hector said. "So, feel free to mess up next time, too. I'll be glad to bail you out of trouble again."

Jamere shook his head. "Next time will be just like this time. Without the bad beginning."

CHAPTER

→ 5 ←

Winning Streak

Jamere kept gaining confidence, and Fairfield kept winning. He scored fifteen points in a big victory over Essex. Then he popped in seventeen as Fairfield routed Memorial.

"First place," Hector said as they walked home after the Memorial game. "All alone on the top of the league. Of course, that depends on winning the next game."

There was only one game left on the schedule. A rematch with Westwood. And Trey Freeman. Fairfield's record was 12–1. Westwood's was 11–2. They'd be tied for first if Westwood won.

"We'll win," Jamere mumbled. "We're playing great."

"Kyle says he can start practicing tomorrow," Hector said.

That was news to Jamere. "So what?" he said. "It's my job now." He'd led the team to three wins. Jamere was sure Coach Sanchez wouldn't bench him. Would he?

"Kyle says he's as good as new," Hector continued.

"And I'm better than ever." Jamere walked faster. He was hungry and didn't feel like worrying about Kyle's return. "It's my job now," he said sharply.

"You said that already."

"So don't forget it." Jamere headed down his street.

Micah was in the kitchen when Jamere entered. He was stirring a pot of pasta.

"Mom working late again?" Jamere asked.

"No, she's here," Micah said. He smiled. "Don't you like my cooking?"

"It's fine." Jamere set his backpack on the table. "We won again."

"Good." Micah pointed to the bag. "We're eating there. Clear your stuff and set the table."

"And congratulations," Micah called as Jamere left the room. "Can't wait to hear about the win."

But Jamere was quiet during dinner. He kept thinking about how Kyle had outplayed him in practice for most of the season. Kyle was the one who had shut down Trey Freeman. With the league title on the line, wouldn't Coach want his best point guard on the court?

"You must be tired," Mom said. "Usually you're yacking away after a game."

"I guess I am tired," Jamere replied.

"You're balancing basketball and books," Mom said. "And doing very well at both. I can understand why you're worn out."

That evening, Jamere's mind kept drifting to the basketball court.

"You all right?" Micah asked.

Jamere shrugged. "Kyle's back tomorrow."

Micah picked up a basketball in the corner of their room. "Let's go shoot some hoops."

Jamere rolled off of his bed and grabbed his Knicks T-shirt. He followed Micah out of the apartment.

The evening was cool and damp, but there was no wind. They headed to the playground two blocks away. The lights from nearby buildings made it just bright enough to see.

Micah always seemed to know when Jamere was upset. Shooting baskets usually changed his mood for the better.

Micah took a jump shot. The metal-chain net rattled as the ball fell through.

"Sounds like you've shown you belong in the starting lineup," Micah said.

"I've earned it," Jamere said. He chased after the ball and sent a swift pass to his brother.

"Coach Sanchez is fair," Micah said. "He benched me a couple of times when I deserved it. For mouthing off or being lazy. But as long as I played hard, he was on my side."

"I always play hard," Jamere said.

"So you have nothing to worry about." Micah bounced the ball to him.

Jamere tossed in a reverse lay-up. "Do you think he'd give the job back to Kyle?"

Micah rebounded the ball. "He'll do what's best for the team. Kyle's coming off an injury. He may be ready to play, but he may be limited. And if I was the coach, I wouldn't mess with a good thing. You've been leading the team. And winning."

Jamere had no idea what Coach would do. But he did feel better. Micah always managed to do that for him.

"You know, having two good point guards is a nice problem for a coach." Micah grinned at him.

"Maybe," Jamere said. "But it's a bad problem for the one who sits on the bench."

"There are lots of minutes to go around."

Jamere knew that. But he didn't want to play half a game. Especially if he had to share time with Kyle.

Jamere took a long shot at the basket. The ball rolled around the rim, then fell in.

"Welcome back, Kyle," Jamere said. "You're in for a battle tomorrow."

CHAPTER
→» 6 «←

Kyle's Return

Jamere was pleased when Coach sent him onto the court with the starters for the next day's scrimmage. He was surprised when Hector joined the second team.

"Guess Kyle's third string now," Jamere whispered. "Right where he belongs."

"Don't be too sure," Hector replied. "Just ignore him and play the game."

Jamere glanced at Kyle. He sat on the bottom row of the bleachers. His ankle was wrapped in a thinner bandage that fit snugly into his sneaker.

After starting three games, Jamere knew his teammates' moves. He could sense when Derek would break into the corner for an open jumper. Or if Lonnie was about to set a screen.

Hector kept up the pressure, guarding Jamere tight. But Jamere was at ease. The starters dominated.

Then Coach waved Kyle onto the court. Hector took a seat.

"Just like old times," Kyle said, standing face-to-face with Jamere.

"Not exactly," Jamere said. He tapped his own chest with a finger. "I'm the starter."

"For now," Kyle replied with a hard glare.

Coach blew his whistle. "Put the ball in play."

Jamere passed to Derek, then raced to the corner. *Let's test that ankle,* he thought.

Even after ten days off, Kyle had no trouble keeping up. He guarded Jamere more tightly than anyone had in the games. He hadn't lost his shooting touch either. Jamere played well, but the second team outplayed the starters. Kyle was the reason why.

"Little break," Coach called. "Get some water."

Coach called Jamere over. "Kyle needs some work with the first team," Coach said. "You've earned a rest, so we'll put Hector back in to cover him."

Make him look bad, Hector, Jamere thought. *Kyle does not deserve my starting job.*

Kyle was two inches taller than Hector and had more muscle. He had little trouble scoring. Kyle was just as fast as before and could cut and spin like always.

Coach stood next to Jamere. "Next basket, go in for Derek," he said.

"Not at point guard?"

"Kyle needs the minutes," Coach said. "Let's see how you two play together."

After Hector made a nice lay-up, Coach stopped the scrimmage. Jamere grabbed the ball.

"My ball," Kyle said, reaching out.

Jamere bounced it to Kyle and ran up the court. "I'm open," he said as Kyle crossed midcourt. Kyle didn't look his way. He dribbled to the other side and passed the ball to Lonnie.

Kyle ignored Jamere every time he brought up the ball. Jamere's only touches were on loose balls or rebounds. The second team tightened its defense, leaving Jamere open much of the time.

And still Kyle didn't pass.

Come on, Jamere thought. *We're not a one-man team, but we're not a four-man team either.* "Pass the ball," he said.

"I've been passing," Kyle said. "To the good players."

The next time Jamere got the ball, he threw it hard at Kyle's bandaged foot. Kyle dodged out of the way.

"At least I can throw an accurate pass," Kyle said.

"That was accurate," Jamere said.

At the end of practice, Coach told the team to sit in the bleachers. "We have one game left," he reminded them. "If we win, we're champions."

"If we lose?" Derek asked.

"Then there'll be a play-off for the title," Coach said. "But we're not thinking about that. We need to beat Westwood. Simple as that."

"Who's starting?" Kyle asked. "As if there should be any doubt."

Jamere clenched his fists and stared at Coach.

Coach let out a short laugh. "There isn't any doubt. Same starting lineup we've had for the past three games. Three wins."

Jamere relaxed. He hadn't lost his job.

"We'll need a team effort to win," Coach said. "Team means passing. Got that, Kyle?"

"I passed plenty," Kyle said.

"Play like a team or expect to sit on the bench," Coach said. "That goes for all of you."

Hector grabbed Jamere's arm as the players headed for the locker room. "Let's shoot a few more free throws," he said.

Jamere knew why Hector wanted him to wait. Kyle would be angry, and a fight wouldn't help anything. He didn't feel like confronting Kyle anyway. Coach had already put Kyle in his place. That was enough for today.

"So," Hector said, "ready for Freeman?" He took a shot, which swished through the net.

"Of course." Jamere hadn't forgotten how badly Freeman outplayed him last time.

"You got what you wanted," Hector said. "Kyle's back, but he's not starting."

"He doesn't deserve to."

Hector dropped in another shot. "He did all right today. Definitely had the edge over me."

Jamere rebounded the ball. Kyle outplayed Jamere today, too. *Only by a little,* he thought. *That's just the flow of the game.*

"Welcome back, right?" Hector said with a sly smile.

Jamere shrugged. "He played all right, I guess. Hogged the ball. Kept up that bad attitude. Like Coach said, if he can't act like a good teammate, he shouldn't be on the court."

"That's the truth," Hector said. He tossed the ball gently at Jamere's foot.

Jamere picked up the ball. "He didn't pass to me at all."

"You shouldn't have aimed at his ankle. You're lucky Coach missed that one," Hector said.

Jamere sighed. "I know. I shouldn't stoop to Kyle's level."

"The best way to keep him in his place is to play great tomorrow," Hector said. "You're still the starter."

"And he's still a pain in the neck."

"Concentrate on Freeman," Hector said. "He's your rival, not Kyle."

Right, Jamere thought. *Let's go win a championship.*

CHAPTER

→ 7 ←

Loud and Rowdy

"This is it," Hector said as Fairfield ran through a lay-up drill before the game.

Jamere tried to concentrate on his shots. He kept looking around the Westwood gym. The bleachers were full of fans in blue-and-yellow shirts. Students cheered each time Trey Freeman made a basket during warm-ups.

Jamere took a pass from Derek and put up a long shot. The ball missed the basket completely.

"Air ball!" shouted some spectators.

The game hasn't even started, and they're already taunting me, Jamere thought.

Coach waved the team to the huddle. "They'll be loud and proud in here all game," he warned. He raised his voice because the Westwood students were stomping their feet and chanting. "This is a tough place to play!"

Freeman strutted onto the court. He shook hands with Jamere but didn't meet his eye. He was a couple of inches taller than Jamere, with broader shoulders.

Relax, Jamere told himself. *Get off to a good start.*

He did. Derek's first pass was on target, and Jamere drained a long shot for a quick 3–0 lead.

The players on the bench jumped up and yelled. But they went quiet again as Freeman matched Jamere's three-pointer with one of his own.

Jamere was tempted to shoot again. Freeman stuck close. Jamere made a swift bounce pass to Lonnie near the basket. Lonnie missed the shot.

Freeman kept making baskets, but Jamere scored again. Fairfield kept things close. Jamere didn't even think about the score. Then Coach called a time-out five minutes into the game.

"Sub!" called Kyle. He pointed to Jamere.

"Already?" Jamere looked at the scoreboard: HOME 11. GUEST 8.

Coach tapped Jamere on the shoulder. "Good work," he said. "Stay ready."

Kyle played the next several minutes and led Fairfield to a small lead. Midway through the second quarter, Coach told Jamere to go back in.

Freeman promptly hit a jumper. Then another.

By halftime, Westwood's lead was back up to three points. Jamere knew Freeman was outplaying him, but not by much.

Jamere started the second half. The margin never got higher than five points. Kyle subbed in for Jamere for a few minutes and led Fairfield back to within a point. Then Coach sent Jamere in, and Freeman made a three-pointer.

Derek fouled out late in the fourth quarter. Jamere wasn't surprised to see Kyle report in.

"Who's at the point?" Jamere called to Coach.

"You," Coach said. "But Kyle will guard Freeman."

Lonnie made a basket. Kyle stole the ball from Freeman and went the length of the court for another. Fairfield had cut the lead to two.

"Less than a minute," Coach said during a time-out. "Tight defense. This game is ours."

The Westwood fans didn't think so. They were making so much noise that Jamere could barely think.

On Fairfield's next possession, Kyle yelled for the ball. Jamere ignored him. He drove hard into the lane and raised the ball to shoot.

Wham! Freeman blocked the shot. Jamere stumbled as the rest of the players ran the other way. Freeman was ahead of everyone with the ball. Kyle raced to stop him.

Jamere could do nothing more than watch as Freeman leaped toward the basket. Kyle twisted to avoid barging into him. They fell to the floor.

The ball went in. The referee blew his whistle.

"Foul," the ref said.

"No way!" Kyle shouted, jumping to his feet.

The crowd taunted Kyle. He walked toward the referee. "I didn't touch him!" he said.

The ref opened one palm and brought the other across in the sign of a *T*. "Technical foul," he said.

Kyle swung at the air. Coach pulled him out of the game and sent in Hector.

Freeman made the first free throw. Then he dropped in another. That was all Westwood needed to wrap up the game.

The Fairfield players tromped out of the gym. *We had them beat*, Jamere thought.

Coach stood in the aisle of the bus as it idled in the parking lot. "Hope you guys liked this place." He gave them a tired smile. "We'll be back here in two days for the play-off game."

Back at school, Coach called Jamere into his office. "So, what do you think?" he asked.

Jamere stared at the door. "I think we should have won."

"So do I," Coach replied. "What could we have done better?"

Jamere met Coach's eyes. "Kyle's dumb technical foul didn't help."

"Who should be our starting point guard?"

"You're asking me?"

Coach nodded.

Jamere leaned his elbows on the desk. "Kyle played well, all right? But I did, too."

Coach agreed. "You both did. But you and Kyle don't play well together. That's a problem."

Jamere sighed.

"We have three options," Coach said. "You've been the starter. And most of the time you're a leader. So I'll let you decide. You can start the game at point guard. Or Kyle can start, and you can come in off the bench later. The third choice is for both of you to start. Kyle would play the point, and you'd start at the other guard spot instead of Derek."

Jamere shut his eyes. He wanted to start. But deep inside he knew Kyle was more effective guarding Freeman. If Freeman got off to a hot start against Jamere again, the game could turn into a blowout. Letting Kyle start would feel like a wimpy move. But it might be better for the team. Having them both start seemed like a good compromise. But would that be fair to Derek?

"Think it over tonight," Coach said. "You can let me know tomorrow."

THE ENDING IS UP2U!

If you think Jamere should face up to his nerves and choose to start at point guard, turn to page 58.

→ OR ←

If you think Jamere should do what's best for the team and let Kyle start, turn to page 66.

→ OR ←

If you think Jamere should take Derek's spot in the starting lineup while letting Kyle start at point guard, turn to page 73.

ENDING
→ 1 ←

Facing His Fear

The players gathered in the locker room before the bus ride back to Westwood.

"Jamere will start," Coach Sanchez said. "He's earned it."

Jamere glanced at Kyle, who was slowly shaking his head. "Then I'll have to bail him out," Kyle muttered.

Jamere told Coach he was ready to face the pressure. He'd succeed or he'd fail. But he wouldn't back away from the challenge.

In the opening minutes, Freeman burned him for three baskets. Jamere knew he had no one to blame but himself. Freeman led Westwood to a 16–5 lead in the first quarter.

It was no surprise when Kyle reported in. Jamere sat on the bench and sighed. His worst fear was coming true.

I knew I should have let Kyle start, he thought. *Too much ego.*

Hector nudged him. "It's early," he said. "We can get back in this."

"If we do, it won't be because of me," Jamere said. He watched the next several minutes in silence.

"Yikes," Hector said as Freeman popped in a fall-away jumper. Westwood's lead had grown to twelve points.

"I'm noticing something," Jamere said. "What happens when Freeman drives to his right?"

Hector shrugged. "He scores."

"When Freeman drives left, he takes the shot if he's open," Jamere said. "But if he's guarded tight, he passes. When he goes right, he never passes."

Less than a minute remained in the half when Jamere replaced Derek. "Force Freeman to his right," Jamere whispered to Kyle. "I'll double up on him."

Freeman passed once, then demanded the ball back. Kyle overplayed his left side, and Freeman drove the opposite way.

Jamere swiped the ball. His long pass led Kyle perfectly. The lay-up cut the lead to ten.

"Nice one," Kyle said. Those were the first positive words he'd said to Jamere all season.

Freeman fell into the same trap again. Jamere deflected the shot. Lonnie grabbed the ball.

"Last shot," Coach yelled.

With four seconds on the clock, Kyle drained a shot from the corner. The Fairfield players ran off the court, trailing 30–22.

"This is our game," Kyle said. "It's ours."

"Not so fast," Coach said. "We made a nice run there, but we have to keep it up. If Freeman's going to be a one-man offense, then he's going to be doubled. I like that adjustment you made, Jamere."

"I've been watching him too long," Jamere said. "Finally figured something out."

Fairfield kept up the double pressure on Freeman. But Freeman was a smart player. Soon he was passing on every drive—right or left. Fairfield chipped away at the lead, but still trailed by five with two minutes remaining in the game.

Coach kept rotating his guards, giving Kyle, Derek, and Jamere short rests. Jamere was on the bench when Kyle drew his fourth foul.

"Jamere and Hector," Coach called. "Get in there."

Hector hadn't played at all. Jamere was surprised he was going in. But Derek looked very tired. And Kyle was in danger of fouling out.

"I'll cover Freeman," Jamere said. "You help out when he drives."

Jamere dribbled up the court. Freeman stuck close, waving his hands. Jamere made a safe pass to Hector.

"Move the ball," Jamere said. He took a return pass, then dribbled to the free throw line and faked a shot. Two players charged toward him. Jamere fired a pass to Hector, who scored.

"Defense, now!" Jamere called.

Freeman raced past midcourt, where Jamere met him. Freeman took a big side step, then darted to his right. Hector slid over to double up. Freeman leaped high and sent a soft, one-handed shot into the basket.

"So we don't stop him every time," Jamere said. Hector bounced the ball to him. "Let's get it back."

"Try to go back door," Hector said. He meant for Jamere to lose Freeman near the basket.

Jamere stood outside the arc and acted like he was too tired to run. He put his hands on his knees while Freeman faced him.

In an instant, Jamere burst toward the basket, keeping a step ahead of Freeman. Hector's pass reached him in the lane. Jamere leaned toward the basket as he shot, taking a hard foul from the Westwood center.

The shot went in.

The Fairfield players leaped and cheered. Kyle reported in for Hector.

"Let's finish this, Jamere," Kyle said. "Make this shot!"

Jamere wiped his face on his jersey. Bounced the ball twice. Made the free throw.

That cut the lead to one point. Thirty-four seconds remained.

"Press!" Jamere called.

He spread his arms to hassle the player trying to make the inbounds pass. The pass went over

Freeman's head. A mad scramble for the ball left four players on the floor. Lonnie tipped it into the air.

Jamere grabbed it. "Time-out!" he called.

"Last shot," Coach said. "We win or lose on this possession."

Kyle grabbed Jamere's arm as they ran out onto the court. "We got this," he said. "You and me. Keep moving. One of us will be open. Doesn't matter which one."

Jamere dribbled. Passed. Cut to the corner. Took another pass from Kyle.

Freeman was in Jamere's face, swiping for the ball. The fans counted down the seconds. "Eight, seven, six . . ."

Jamere saw a narrow opening along the baseline. He drove and leaped, but even then he hadn't made a decision. Shoot, or . . .

Kyle was wide open at the free throw line. Jamere tossed him the ball.

Kyle nailed the shot.
Fairfield won the title!

ENDING
→ 2 ←
Best for the Team?

Jamere took a deep breath. "I think it's best for the team if Kyle starts," he told Coach. "He's a better defender against Freeman."

"That's true," Coach said. "This is your decision to make. But this is just between you and me, Jamere."

"I decided to swallow my pride," Jamere said. "If it was anybody but Kyle, I'd feel better about this. But I shouldn't hurt the team because he's a jerk."

Coach laughed. "You'll play plenty. Freeman has enough energy to tire out two point guards."

Kyle made a few sharp remarks during the warm-up about Jamere losing his starting job.

"Ignore him," Hector said.

"Seems like you tell me that every day," Jamere replied.

Freeman played a different style today. Instead of looking to shoot on every possession, he ran the offense like a quarterback. Several pinpoint passes led to easy lay-ups by the center. Westwood built an early lead.

Kyle missed four shots midway through the first quarter. "Let's see if you can do better," Coach said to Jamere. "Freeman's picking us apart."

Jamere scowled at Kyle as he took his place on the court. Kyle looked away.

I'll give us a spark, Jamere thought. *Kyle might never get off that bench again.*

But Jamere missed his first two shots. Freeman continued his sharp offensive play. He took the open shots. He also relied more on smart passing. Westwood built the lead to double digits.

"They're simply outplaying us," Coach said at the half. He pointed at Kyle, then Jamere. "You two. The only way we can win this game is if both of you are out there. Playing together. If you act like rivals, we'll get run out of this gym. If you act like teammates, we'll have a chance."

Jamere hung back while the others went to the court. "Kyle," he said.

Kyle stepped closer and stared.

"We should double-team him sometimes," Jamere said. "Force him to take a bad shot."

Kyle nodded. "Look for me making some sharp cuts," he said. "He'll be expecting me to run the offense. Maybe I can shake loose for an open lay-up."

But Fairfield had dug a deep hole. Kyle's back-door lay-up idea worked once. And, they managed to force Freeman into an off-balance shot that missed. But the lead stayed between five and eight points throughout the second half.

"We need one big run," Coach said during a time-out. He had to shout to be heard above the spectators. They were stomping their feet and chanting "West-WOOD" over and over.

Jamere looked up at the scoreboard. 40–34. 1:38. 4Q.

Kyle shadowed Freeman, making him stop his dribble and force a risky pass. Lonnie grabbed the ball and tossed it to Jamere.

Patience, Jamere told himself. *Plenty of time.*

He and Kyle passed back and forth, dribbling in and out. Finally Jamere cut into the lane. Kyle passed the ball, and Jamere immediately fired it back.

Kyle made the three-point shot.

Freeman scored again to make it 42–37. The spectators leaped to their feet. They stayed like that for the rest of the game.

Jamere set a screen and Kyle eased by. He flipped the ball to Lonnie for a lay-up.

"Press!" Jamere yelled as he hounded his opponent. Freeman tried to pass the ball safely.

Kyle tipped the pass. Jamere raced toward the bouncing ball. He took it in stride and dribbled to the basket. His lay-up cut the lead to a point.

Freeman called a time-out.

Jamere leaped into the air. Kyle raised his fist as they ran to the bench.

"Make them earn it," Coach said. "If they score two, we hold for a final three-pointer. If we get a stop, then one basket will win us the title."

"Let's go!" Jamere said as he joined Kyle on the court. Finally, they were playing like teammates. The championship was right there for the taking.

Jamere stuck to his opponent, keeping an eye on Freeman, too. The seconds ticked away.

The ball went inside. Kyle and Jamere crashed in to stop a lay-up.

But the ball flew back to the top of the key.

Freeman easily made the three-pointer.

The fans counted down the final seconds. Kyle's three-point shot at the other end wasn't enough.

The final buzzer sounded. Game over.

They'd come so close.

Jamere sat down hard on the bench, with Kyle next to him.

Jamere wiped his forehead with his wrist. "Why didn't we work together like that all game?" he whispered.

Kyle shut his eyes. "Why not all season?" he asked.

Jamere looked out at the court. Freeman was being mobbed by the spectators. "Yeah," Jamere said, slowly shaking his head. "Why not?"

"We'll do better next season," Kyle said.

Jamere nodded. He liked the sound of that.

ENDING
→ 3 ←

Teamwork

The Westwood gym was even rowdier than last time. Jamere did his best to tune it out. He felt loose and confident.

Coach Sanchez had agreed with Jamere's decision to have Kyle play point guard and cover Freeman. Jamere would start, too, but with less pressure at the other guard spot.

"Kyle better not freeze me out this time." Jamere bounced the ball to Hector. "This game is too important."

"That cuts both ways," Hector said. "You have to work with him, too. Pass the ball."

"I'm not the problem," Jamere insisted.

Hector rolled his eyes. "He's most of the problem. But you're part of it."

Lonnie won the opening jump and tapped the ball to Kyle. Jamere was surprised to see that Freeman was guarding him. *Maybe he thinks I'll be playing the point,* he thought. But Freeman continued to cover Jamere after several possessions, even though Kyle covered Freeman when Westwood had the ball.

Both teams were ice-cold. Westwood called a time-out midway through the first quarter. The game was tied, 2–2.

"Great defense so far," Coach said. "Keep shooting. The shots will go in."

Jamere hadn't taken a shot yet. Freeman had guarded him tightly. The best Jamere could do was to set screens for the others and make a few passes.

Kyle poked Jamere's shoulder. Jamere turned.

"Cut to the basket," Kyle whispered. "Try to get a jump on Freeman."

Jamere nodded. He might catch Freeman off guard with a quick cut inside.

Freeman finally made a shot to give Westwood the lead. Jamere hung back on offense, passing back and forth with Kyle. Then he stood still for a second, acting lazy, before darting toward the hoop.

Kyle sent a perfect bounce pass into the lane. Jamere scooped it up. He made a lay-up, despite getting fouled from behind by Freeman.

"Smart move, Jamere!" Coach called.

It was a good move. But Jamere knew the "smarts" had come from Kyle. Jamere made the free throw.

Freeman hit a couple of jumpers. Now that Jamere wasn't covering him, he'd noticed something about Freeman's style. When play stopped for a free throw, Jamere waved Kyle over.

"Freeman doesn't like to go to his left," Jamere said. "Force him in that direction. I'll help out."

The strategy worked. Twice Kyle overplayed Freeman to one side, not letting him drive to the right. The first time, Jamere stole the ball. The second, Freeman missed an off-balance shot.

"Not as loud in here as last time." Jamere turned to Coach during a rest.

"That's because we're outplaying them," Coach said. "Don't worry. It'll get loud again."

Coach was right. When Freeman hit a long three-pointer, the fans erupted in cheers. They grew even louder when he sped past Kyle for a lay-up.

"I think Kyle's hobbling," Jamere said.

"I think so, too. Report in."

Jamere kneeled by the scorer's table until the next whistle. "Ankle okay?" he asked Kyle.

"No problem," Kyle said. But then he winced in pain.

Kyle stayed on the bench for the rest of the half. Westwood led by three points at the break.

"Kyle's done," Coach said. "Can't risk a worse injury to that ankle. So Jamere, Derek, and Hector, the guard play is all up to you."

Kyle waved Jamere and the guards toward him as they left the locker room. "He's not Superman," Kyle said, referring to Freeman. "But he'll always take a shot if he can. Double up on him. Force him to take bad shots."

Kyle grabbed Jamere's jersey and held him back. "You've got this," he said. "Freeman's going to score, but you can limit him."

"Thanks," Jamere said. "How bad is the ankle?"

"It'll be all right," Kyle said. "But not today. This one's up to you."

Jamere guarded Freeman throughout the second half. Whenever Freeman slipped away, Derek was there to help. But Freeman didn't pass to an open player. He ducked his head and tried to drive. Jamere stole the ball twice. Fairfield built a lead.

Kyle's advice had paid off.

Less than a minute remained in the game. Fairfield led, 45–33, and had wrapped up the championship.

Jamere finally left the court for a rest. He walked along the bench, shaking hands with his teammates. When he got to Kyle, they both let out a laugh.

"No more weak links," Kyle said. "Great game, Jamere."

"No more annoying jerks, either," Jamere said. "Just champions. And teammates."

Write Your Own Ending

There were three endings to choose from in *Backcourt Battle*. Did you find the ending you wanted from the story? Or did you want something different to happen? Now it is your turn! Write the ending you would like to see. Be creative!